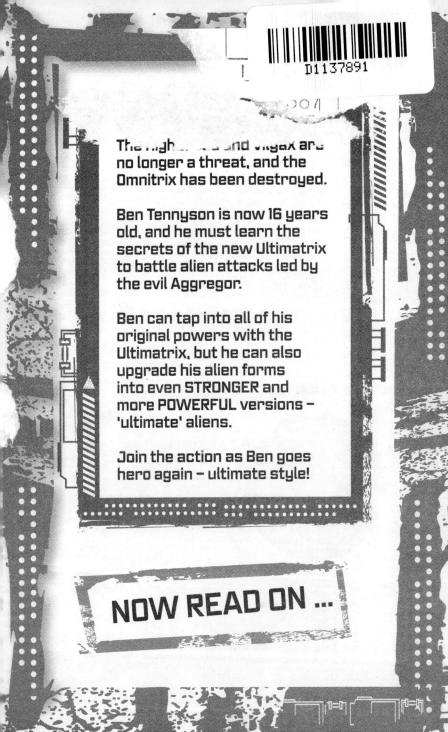

The High... and Vilgax are no longer a threat, and the Omnitrix has been destroyed.

Ben Tennyson is now 16 years old, and he must learn the secrets of the new Ultimatrix to battle alien attacks led by the evil Aggregor.

Ben can tap into all of his original powers with the Ultimatrix, but he can also upgrade his alien forms into even STRONGER and more POWERFUL versions – 'ultimate' aliens.

Join the action as Ben goes hero again – ultimate style!

NOW READ ON ...

MEET THE CHARACTERS

Ben Tennyson
Back for more superhero action

Gwen Tennyson
Ben's cousin, with powers of her own

Kevin E. Levin
He lends some serious muscle

Julie Yamamoto
Ben's girlfriend

Humungousaur
A huge dinosaur alien

Jet Ray
A flying, swimming and stinging alien

ChromaStone
This crystal guy is razor sharp

Spidermonkey
Very agile and can spin webs

Ultimate Spidermonkey

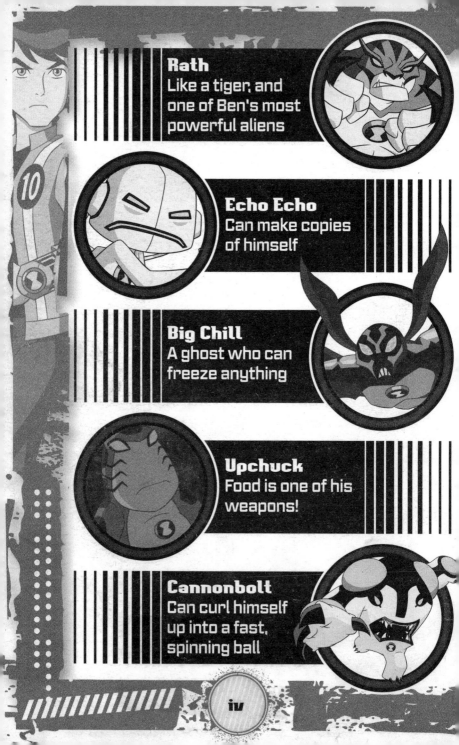

Rath
Like a tiger, and one of Ben's most powerful aliens

Echo Echo
Can make copies of himself

Big Chill
A ghost who can freeze anything

Upchuck
Food is one of his weapons!

Cannonbolt
Can curl himself up into a fast, spinning ball

Lodestar
He's a real magnetic guy

Will Harangue
A power-crazy TV presenter

Bivalvan
One of four aliens kidnapped by Aggregor

Aggregor
A villain who can absorb the power of aliens

Forever Knights
Dangerous collectors of illegal alien tech

EGMONT

We bring stories to life

First published in Great Britain 2011
by Egmont UK Limited
239 Kensington High Street
London W8 6SA

CARTOON NETWORK, the logo, BEN 10 ULTIMATE ALIEN
and all related characters and elements are trademarks
of and © 2011 Cartoon Network.

Adapted by Barry Hutchison

ISBN 978 1 4052 5704 6

47563/2

Printed and bound in Great Britain

The Forest Stewardship Council (FSC) is an international,
non-governmental organisation dedicated to promoting responsible
management of the world's forests. FSC operates a system of forest
certification and product labelling that allows consumers to identify
wood and wood-based products from well-managed forests.

For more information about Egmont's paper buying policy,
please visit www.egmont.co.uk/ethicalpublishing
For more information about the FSC, please visit
their website at www.fsc.org

C015898900

FAME

CHAPTER ONE

TV STAR

Ben, Gwen and Kevin were watching TV at Ben's house. Their mouths were hanging open in shock.

'There are aliens among us,' announced a newsreader. The screen showed the gooey green form of Goop, one of Ben's amazing alien heroes.

The image then changed to show Wildmutt racing into battle, and then Echo Echo.

'Strange creatures, with unbelievable powers,' the newsreader continued.

Flash. Another change of

shot. Jet Ray swooping low over the ocean.

Flash. Cannonbolt, smashing through a concrete pillar.

Flash. The shot changed again. Ben looked at the figure on screen and groaned. It was him!

'All of the creatures you've just seen actually come from one man. His name is Ben Tennyson.'

Kevin flashed Ben a grin. 'You are *so* busted.'

Gwen jabbed a button on the remote, changing the channel. The story, though, was exactly the same. Images of Humungousaur lifting a bridge; ChromaStone smashing into a parked van. Aliens, aliens, aliens.

'Every channel, Ben,' Gwen said. 'Showing nothing but you wrecking things. And they know who you are!'

Sighing, Ben stood up. He crossed the room and opened the front door. Dozens of cameras flashed in his face, almost blinding him. He slammed the door closed just as a crowd of journalists rushed forward, calling his name.

Ben thought for a moment, and then smiled. If it was an alien they wanted, it was an alien they were going to get.

The reporters looked up excitedly as the front door of Ben's house swung open and Ben himself stepped out. They raced towards him, shouting questions.

A microphone was thrust in front of Ben's mouth. 'Mr Tennyson,' asked the reporter holding it, 'do you have a statement?'

'Yeah,' Ben smiled, twisting the dial of his alien watch, the Ultimatrix. 'It's hero time!'

WHOOSH!

A swirling cloud of green wrapped around Ben and the crowd watched as the harmless-looking boy suddenly transformed into a huge dinosaur-like creature.

'Humungousaur!' he boomed, raising both fists to the sky. Then he let out a long, deafening roar.

Screaming, the terrified crowd ran for their lives. Humungousaur kept roaring for as long as he could, and then he transformed back into human form. Gwen and Kevin hurried out to join him.

'You should have used one of your new Ultimate transformations,' said Kevin.

Ben frowned and looked down at the watch. He'd had to sacrifice the Omnitrix in his battle with his evil double, Albedo, but he'd ended up with something even more powerful – the Ultimatrix. The only problem was, he wasn't quite sure how it worked.

'I wanted to scare *them*,' Ben mumbled. 'Not *me*.'

Later on, Ben was hanging out with his girlfriend, Julie, at her house. They had the TV on, and Will Harangue, a man with greying hair and thick glasses was scowling into the camera.

'Welcome back to the Will Harangue Nation,' he said. 'Our top story has to be Ben Tennyson, a sixteen-year-old high school student who has been outed as a one-man alien invasion.'

The presenter's voice droned on. The picture changed to show several clips of Ben's aliens accidentally destroying public property.

'... we now know that all of these random attacks –'

'Attacks?' Ben yelped.

'– were the work of Ben Tennyson, for who knows what sinister purpose?'

Ben was furious. 'How about saving the whole entire universe? How's *that* for sinister?'

Click.

The screen went dark as Julie hit the off button on the remote. 'It's too sunny to be sitting inside,' she said. 'Let's go for a drive in your car. That always cheers you up!'

'I don't *need* cheering up,' Ben said, folding his arms across his chest. 'I'm not upset.'

Julie looked at him. 'Why not?' she joked. 'Everybody hates you!'

CHAPTER TWO

THE MASTERMIND

A green and black car prowled along, leading away from the town of Bellwood. Ben was behind the wheel and Julie was sitting in the passenger seat. She was right. Getting out in the car had cheered him up.

Suddenly, another car cut across in front of them, forcing Ben to slam down on the brakes. With a sharp **screeeech**, he brought his car to a stop right beside the other one. He rolled down his window, just as the driver of the other car did the same.

Ben glared at Kevin. 'What's

the emergency?'

'While you guys have been hiding from reporters, I've been *working*,' Kevin told them. 'I found the guy who figured out your secret identity, then blabbed it all over the internet,' he told Ben. 'I say we pay him a visit.'

Ben screwed the fingers of one hand into a tight fist, then punched it hard into the palm of his other hand. 'Best idea I've heard all day.'

It was dark by the time Ben, Gwen and Kevin had found the right street. They stood on the path outside an old block of flats.

The front door was ajar and Kevin wasted no time in pushing it wide open and stomping inside.

A flight of stairs was just inside the hallway, and Kevin headed up, with Gwen and Ben following behind.

Kevin nodded in the direction of a wooden door at the top of the stairs. 'The guy in there's the *mastermind*. We've got to be ready for anything!'

Gwen rolled her eyes and pushed past the boys. Raising her hand, she rapped hard on the door.

With a **creak**, the door inched open. An eye peered out at them, moving across them slowly. Finally, the eye settled on Ben's jacket.

The door opened fully and a woman stood in the doorway. 'You must be friends of James,' she said, softly. Then she turned her head and roared 'Jiiiiimmmmmy!' in a voice that shook the walls.

'I'm *coming*, mum!'

There was a clattering noise from inside the flat, and a boy of around ten-years-old appeared beside the woman. The boy wore a homemade copy of Ben's green jacket and a white t-shirt.

Gwen glanced at Kevin and tried not to laugh. '*That's* your mastermind?'

'Ben Tennyson!' the boy gasped. 'I'm Jimmy Jones. It's so *great* to meet you!'

Ben and Gwen stood in Jimmy's bedroom, staring in amazement at the walls. It was covered with photographs of Ben and his alien forms, newspaper cuttings and maps.

Kevin wasn't interested in the walls, though. 'Why did you do this to Ben?' he snarled, grabbing Jimmy by his jacket and hoisting him off the ground.

'I don't understand!' Jimmy whimpered. 'Do what?'

'Ruin his life!'

'I would never do anything to hurt Mr Tennyson,' Jimmy protested. 'I'm a fan!'

Kevin hesitated, then grunted and let Jimmy fall down onto his bed. Almost immediately, the boy's eyes filled with tears.

Jimmy sniffed and looked across at Ben. 'I am very sorry, Mr Tennyson.'

Ben sat on the bed beside the boy and handed him a tissue. 'Why did you post that video?' he asked.

Jimmy blew his nose loudly. 'I run a website,' he said. 'I collect pictures of aliens that people have taken. I noticed that a lot of them came from Bellwood.'

He moved over to the laptop on his desk. There were several

pictures of Ben's aliens on the computer screen.

'So I started sorting the pictures. Lots of them were wearing this symbol,' he said, pointing to the Omnitrix on Swampfire's chest.

Gwen knew what was coming next. 'And you pieced together Ben's identity from a picture of him wearing the Omnitrix.'

'Yeah! I found stories all over the internet about how you helped people and saved the world,' Jimmy said. 'I just thought everybody should know how cool you are.'

'We know you were trying to help, but by revealing Ben's secret, you've made it harder for him to help people,' Gwen explained.

Jimmy hung his head. 'I'm sorry. I thought you'd like the fame.

I've got pictures of a lot of your alien forms,' he said. 'Humungousaur, Goop, Jeffrey ...'

'"Jeffrey"?' laughed Ben. 'You thought I named one of my aliens "Jeffrey"? It's "Jet Ray"!'

Jimmy blushed. 'That does make more sense.'

Gwen was looking at another photo on the wall. She pointed at a picture of a large, menacing alien. 'Who,' she asked, 'is this one?'

CHAPTER THREE

UP, UP AND AWAY!

All four children were on their feet, studying the picture on the wall.

'I just assumed that it was Mr Tennyson,' Jimmy said. 'It first showed up a few months ago. All of the sightings have been in Orlando. Hang on, I've got some video.'

On his laptop he brought up some security camera film taken from inside a military aircraft building. It showed armed guards firing lasers at the red alien. The blasts bounced harmlessly off its tough, shell-like armour. Ben watched in amazement as the alien

17

raised its hands and knocked the guards clean off their feet with high-powered blasts of water from its palms.

Ben turned to Gwen and Kevin. 'Fancy a road trip?'

'We'll take the Rustbucket,' replied Kevin.

Ben snorted. 'You want to drive all the way to Florida?'

Kevin grinned. 'Not that Rustbucket. The new one.'

Ben's car prowled through an old airfield, past the rusting remains of several old aeroplanes. Gwen sat beside him in the passenger seat. They both looked left and right, searching for any sign of –

'Whoa!' Ben gasped, as he

spotted the sleek green aircraft standing in the darkness ahead of them. It looked like something from a science-fiction movie, all sharp lines and gleaming metal. The Rustbucket III.

'Nice, huh?' Kevin's voice came at them from the two-way radio in Gwen's Plumber badge. 'It was a standard Plumber-issue ship, but I've made some improvements.'

A ramp lowered from beneath the jet. Ben drove his car up into the plane's belly. Once inside, he and

Gwen rushed to meet up with Kevin in the cockpit.

'Specs?' Ben asked, eagerly.

Kevin swivelled in the pilot's seat. 'Supersonic in atmosphere, subspace hyperdrive for effective FTL. Bonus gizmos I've acquired here and there.'

Ben was almost drooling. 'Sweet!'

'Extranet access!' chirped Gwen, sitting down at a computer screen. 'We can use our Plumber's badges to access any database on Earth, even secure ones.'

Ben tried to fight back a yawn, but failed. 'Boring,' he said, then turned to Kevin. 'Make it go!'

Kevin spun back to the controls. Beneath them, the engines of the Rustbucket III roared into life, and Gwen and Ben hurried to strap themselves into their seats.

A split-second later, with the rocket thrusters spitting orange flames, the plane lifted off and rocketed up into the night sky.

'I found the source of the video,' Gwen said, when the roar of the engines had died down. 'Security cameras in a top secret NASA facility. I'm sending you the coordinates, Kevin.'

'Got 'em,' nodded Kevin, as the details came through on his

screen. 'We should be there in two minutes.'

RWOOOO! RWOOOO!

A warning light on the control panel began to flash a furious red. On the radar, three flashing blips were approaching fast.

'Trouble,' said Kevin. 'We're flying into restricted air space.'

Up ahead, three fighter jets screamed through the air towards them, their weapons ready to fire. Kevin pulled the Rustbucket III into a steep climb.

Too late! A burst of energy streaked from the third fighter jet and slammed into the underside of the Rustbucket, sending it into a sharp, sudden dive.

'This is a brand new paint job!' Kevin growled, bringing the plane level again. He pressed a red button and an energy beam fired from the Rustbucket's weapons systems. The beam sliced through the third jet fighter, cutting it in half. As it began to fall, the cockpit flew open and the pilot ejected to safety with a parachute.

'Kevin!' Gwen hissed. 'Those guys are on our side. You can't shoot at them!'

'No harm done. He ejected,' said Kevin. He glanced out of the window and suddenly he turned pale and looked very nervous.

Ben followed Kevin's gaze. The pilot was plummeting towards the ground and his parachute had almost completely burned away.

Ben ran over to a circular hatch on the floor. 'Open it,' he barked. Kevin punched a button on the controls and the floor beneath Ben slid away.

For a moment, Ben seemed to hang in mid-air, and then he was falling, dropping like a stone towards the Earth.

Struggling against the wind, Ben slammed his hand down on the Ultimatrix and was instantly transformed into the flying alien Jet Ray. Folding his wings in tight by his sides, he rocketed after the plummeting pilot.

Jet Ray closed in on the man in seconds. He was ready to catch him, but a series of blasts screamed past, forcing Jet Ray to turn sharply.

The other two planes were firing their weapons, trying to keep the alien away from their colleague.

They think I'm attacking him! thought Jet Ray, and he quickly vanished into the clouds, out of sight of the jets.

'He's gone!' one of the pilots barked into his radio. And then, 'There he is! *There he –*'

A scorching beam of red energy sliced through both planes. Inside, the pilots jammed their fingers against their triggers, but the weapons didn't work. Meanwhile, Jet Ray was racing towards the ground.

'Got you!' he cried, catching the falling pilot with just seconds to spare.

Touching down, Jet Ray released the stunned pilot. Jet Ray was ready to take off again, but the click of weapons being loaded stopped him. He was surrounded by twelve armed soldiers.

'Um ... take me to your leader?' he joked.

The closest soldier flashed him an angry sneer. 'If you so much as twitch, you're in trouble.'

Jet Ray raised his arms. 'Easy, guys,' he said. With a flash of green energy, he turned back into human form. 'I'm the famous Ben Tennyson. I'm a superhero. You *have* heard of me, right?'

CLANG!

The barred door of a prison cell slammed shut, trapping Ben inside. A key turned in the lock and he watched the prison guard march off along the corridor.

'Hey!' he cried. 'I'm pretty sure I'm supposed to get a phone call!'

But the guard kept walking, and Ben was left all alone in his cramped, dark prison cell.

CHAPTER FOUR

WATER FIGHT

Ben had been locked up for over an hour. He was just thinking about going alien and smashing his way out, when two familiar faces appeared at his prison cell door.

It was Gwen and Kevin, and behind them was a soldier and his commanding officer.

'Let him out,' barked the colonel, and the soldier rushed to unlock the cell.

Ben looked at Gwen, amazed. 'How did you …?'

'We showed him these,' Gwen replied, holding up her Plumber's badge.

'Even though the Plumbers are secret, every government on Earth knows that you are experts in these matters,' the colonel told him.

'Turns out NASA has a problem,' Kevin explained.

The colonel led them out of the prison block and they followed him to a large aircraft building. They looked up at a sleek space craft.

'It's called the Orion,' the colonel explained. 'It's powered by nuclear energy and can travel at fifteen percent of the speed of light.

Once clear of the Earth, a series of atomic bombs go off, propelling the ship through space.'

'Whoa!' gasped Ben.

'We've been building her for over fifty years. But now it's almost finished, a series of robberies has practically shut us down.'

'Robberies?' said Gwen.

The colonel hesitated, as if he couldn't believe what he was about to say. 'A creature comes in here every night and steals pieces of the ship. Nothing we've tried can stop it.' He looked around the group. 'I'm hoping that maybe you kids will have more luck.'

Night had fallen, casting the building into near-darkness. Up in the gloom near the ceiling, three figures were waiting. Ben, Gwen and Kevin had their eyes fixed on the shadowy outline of the Orion.

KABOOM!

One of the walls suddenly exploded in a shower of dust and rock. Then the alien that the gang had seen on screen in Jimmy's bedroom forced its way inside.

From the top of its head to the base of its spine, it was covered in a rigid, lobster-like shell. Although the heroes didn't yet know it, the alien was known as Bivalvan. And right now, it was heading straight for the Orion.

Gwen moved first, forming a series of floating energy steps in the air, leading down to the alien. Kevin followed, then Ben, who was struggling with the Ultimatrix.

'Uncatalogued DNA detected,' it chimed. Ben slapped his hand against it. 'Function not available,' it told him. 'Please stand by.'

The others were having more luck. Kevin and Gwen were both on the ground, racing towards Bivalvan, who had already begun tearing equipment from the Orion.

Brushing his fingertips against the concrete floor, Kevin transformed his body into living rock. He swung his stone fists in a wide arc and caught the alien under the chin, sending him rocketing backwards.

With a **CRASH** of metal, Bivalvan smashed into a control console. Gwen and Kevin loomed over him.

'Who are you?' Gwen demanded. 'What do you –?'

The roar of rushing water silenced her. Two powerful jets spat from Bivalvan's hands, striking Gwen and Kevin on the chest. The force of the water tossed them through the air. They hit the ground hard and lay there, dazed, as the alien slowly stalked closer.

Its shadow fell across Gwen. Its narrow eyes seemed to shimmer as it raised one claw-like hand.

'Hey, seafood salad!' cried a voice. 'Over here!'

Bivalvan spun to find Ben hurtling towards him. He was clinging to a chain that dangled from the ceiling, and swinging towards the armoured alien.

THUD!

'Oof!'

Ben rebounded painfully off Bivalvan's chest and landed in a heap on the warehouse floor. The alien glared down, completely unharmed.

'In my head, that worked a lot

better,' Ben groaned.

Bivalvan hissed angrily. Reacting fast, Ben slammed his hand down on the Ultimatrix.

'Function not available,' it said again, cheerfully. 'Please stand by.'

'Aw, man!' Ben cried. He smiled at the alien as he struggled back to his feet. 'I don't suppose you want to talk about this?'

THWACK!

Bivalvan's claw swatted Ben aside, sending him crashing back down onto the floor. With a grunt, the alien turned and began picking up the equipment he'd dropped when Kevin had punched him.

On Ben's wrist, the Ultimatrix blinked a brilliant yellow as a wide beam of light shone from it. It swept up and down Bivalvan's body, from

his armoured head down to his
pointed toes.

'Unknown DNA sample
acquired,' the Ultimatrix announced.
'Scan complete.'

'What did you do?' the alien
demanded, angrily.

'Oh, *now* you want to talk,'
Ben replied. With a bleep, the light
on the watch turned green. He
slammed his hand down and an
amazing transformation took place.

'ChromaStone!' he cried.
'Wasn't sure I still had this one.'

Raising his crystal hands, ChromaStone fired an energy beam at Bivalvan. It hit him hard but didn't knock him over. With a growl, Bivalvan blasted streams of water from his hands. They hit the floor, then curved up into a tidal wave.

ChromaStone winced as he saw the wave rushing towards him. 'You gotta be kidding m–'

That was as far as he got. The wave swept him off his feet and carried him across the room. ChromaStone turned in time to see an electricity generator looming behind him. He tried to scramble to safety, but it was no use. As the water hit the generator, a deadly arc of electricity struck him. He roared in pain as the high voltage shock ran through his body.

With a final **crackle** of electric power, the generator stopped. ChromaStone remained standing for a few seconds, then slowly toppled backwards, unconscious, into the icy cold puddle on the floor.

Ben's eyelids hurt when he tried to open them. But then, the rest of him hurt, too, so he opened his eyes anyway. Gwen, Kevin and the colonel looked down at him. They were blurry at first, but a few blinks brought them into focus.

'Ben? Are you OK?' Gwen asked, worried for her cousin.

Coughing, Ben slowly sat up. The whole room seemed to be spinning, but with Kevin's help, he managed to stand.

'We've got a big problem, son,' the colonel said. 'The first few times that thing came here it stole shielding, a control system, timing sequencers ...'

'But this time?' asked Gwen.

The colonel took a deep breath. He was trembling. 'This time he took the engine.'

Ben felt his stomach go tight. 'And by engine, you mean ...'

'Yes, son,' said the colonel, giving a single nod of his head. 'A nuclear bomb.'

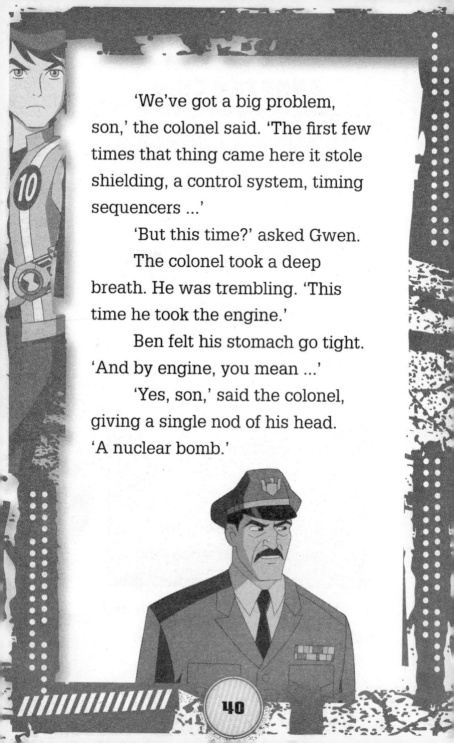

CHAPTER FIVE

UNDER THE SEA

A shimmering ball of pink energy swished through the water, plunging deep beneath the waves. Inside, Ben and Kevin kept their eyes peeled for trouble, while Gwen concentrated on steering and on not crashing into the rocky ocean floor beneath them.

The Rustbucket's sensors had told them they'd find the stolen bomb in an undersea cave. Gwen guided the bubble towards it. With a wave of her fingers, she steered it through the entrance, and back up onto dry land.

The energy bubble fizzled away, leaving them standing inside a dark, damp cave. Large, pointed stalactites hung from the ceiling, dripping water onto the uneven ground below.

Moving quietly, they soon found what they were looking for. Bivalvan was standing with his back to them, using a long, snaking energy cable to weld the Orion's engine onto another spaceship.

'Now I get it,' Ben whispered. 'He's doing the same thing you always do, Kevin.'

Ben stepped out from the

shadows and into Bivalvan's line of sight. 'I think he's just trying to fix up his own ship,' he said, loudly. 'Am I right?'

The alien didn't stop working. 'You are correct. Now leave me be,' he snapped. 'I want to go home, and I am two minutes from launch.'

He flicked a switch on the side of the engine, and a timer began counting down from two minutes.

Gwen stepped forwards. 'If you launch your ship, the explosion will destroy all of Florida!'

Bivalvan shrugged his armoured shoulders. 'I don't see your point.'

'Killing a couple of million people isn't cool,' Kevin said.

Bivalvan turned to face them. The cable in his hands fizzled and crackled with electricity. 'You would stand in my way?' he demanded.

Before anyone could answer, he tossed the cable towards them. Ben rolled sideways to safety and Gwen brought a shield up around Kevin and herself, just in time. The energy field sparked and hissed as the cable struck it.

'That cable's live,' Gwen cried. 'If I drop the shield, it'll fry us!'

There was a flash of green energy as Ben quickly activated the Ultimatrix.

'Spidermonkey!' he cried, as he became the six-limbed alien chimp. He reached for the cable.

'Don't touch it!' Kevin warned, and Spidermonkey pulled away.

'Stop the clam-guy,' Gwen urged. 'We'll think of something.'

Meanwhile, the bomb's timer was counting down. The gang had just over a minute-and-a-half until Bivalvan's ship would blast off, causing a massive explosion.

Spidermonkey backflipped towards Bivalvan. 'A face full of web will slow you down,' he said. With a twitch of his tail, he fired a webline towards Bivalvan's eyes.

But the armoured alien caught hold of the web and yanked on it, pulling the stunned Spidermonkey towards him.

'There is *nothing* you can do to stop me,' Bivalvan barked, driving Spidermonkey further back with a jet of water. With a sneer, he turned and headed for his ship.

'Maybe not *me*,' Spidermonkey admitted. 'But my new Ultimatrix

comes with some new features.'
He tapped a long finger against the
emblem on his chest. 'There's a
time to go hero ... and a time to
go ultimate!'

An amazing change swept
across the alien. His thin body
became bulkier and heavier. Two of
his limbs sunk into his chest, while
the remaining arms and legs grew
thicker and stronger. In seconds, he
had gone from a spindly monkey to
an enormous, six-eyed gorilla.

Roaring, he raised his arms.
The black fur at his sides split open
as he sprouted four long, metal legs.
Their pointed tips slammed down,
raising him high into the air.

'*Ultimate Spidermonkey!*' he
bellowed, pounding his chest with
his powerful fists.

Scurrying forwards, Ultimate Spidermonkey punched Bivalvan's head. The red alien staggered backwards. Shakily, he raised his hands and fired some water blasts.

Ultimate Spidermonkey dodged from side to side, easily avoiding the blasts. Behind him, Kevin thudded a shoulder against the inside of Gwen's energy bubble, causing it to roll safely clear of the welding cable.

Lunging, the powerful Ultimate Spidermonkey wrapped

his mighty arms around Bivalvan's chest. Raising up on his metal legs, he held the struggling alien high off the ground.

'Give up?' he growled.

A creepy grin spread across Bivalvan's face. 'Why should I?'

With a gloopy *schlop* sound, Ultimate Spidermonkey's bottom jaw split in two. Bivalvan screamed as a torrent of sticky webbing erupted from the hero's throat. In just a few moments Bivalvan's whole body was cocooned, leaving only his head free.

'The bomb!' cried the spider-ape, realising the danger was far from over.

'On it!' Kevin cried. He raced to the timer and flipped open the controls. There were two wires inside, one red, one blue. Kevin didn't know which one to pull. In the end, he pulled both and hoped for the best.

With a **beep**, the timer froze at 00:10. Kevin wiped sweat from his brow and grinned. 'With just ten seconds to spare!'

With a flash of green, Ultimate Spidermonkey turned back to his normal Spidermonkey form. Another flash and he was back to being Ben. His eyes glowed a red colour, just for a moment.

'You OK?' Gwen asked.

'Yeah,' replied Ben, steadying himself. 'That's a little ... different.'

Shaking his head clear, he turned to face Bivalvan. The alien was still cocooned, and dangling from a stalactite by a length of web.

'Time for you to start talking,' Ben told him. 'Let's start with your name.'

'I am Bivalvan,' he said. 'I come from a small planet in the Andromeda galaxy.'

'Long way from home,' Kevin said. 'What brings you here?'

'I was kidnapped, along with four others, by a monster named Aggregor,' he replied. 'We managed to escape him, but crashed here on your planet.'

'Well then, where are the

others?' asked Gwen.

'I don't know. We were separated.'

Ben smiled, excited. 'Four aliens that aren't in the Ultimatrix. That's pretty cool.'

'Don't worry about your friends,' Gwen said, stepping closer to Bivalvan. 'We'll find them and get them all a ride back home.'

'And what about me?'

'Same deal,' Ben told him. 'I'll call the Plumbers. They'll take you.'

Just then, a loud tearing of metal echoed around the cave. Ben turned to find Kevin, now in metal form, tearing the bomb away from the side of the ship.

'We'll make sure the bomb gets back to NASA,' Ben said.

'Not that we don't trust you,' Kevin added. 'But we don't.'

Next morning, Ben stood outside a large wooden door, nervously shuffling his feet. He didn't even notice Julie approach.

'You have to go in sometime,' she said, nodding towards the entrance to the school.

'I could drop out,' Ben suggested.

'Ben, last night you were two

feet from an atomic bomb. You *can't* be scared of your classmates.'

Ben sighed. 'Everybody knows my secret, Julie. And if they've been watching the news, everybody hates me.'

Standing on her tiptoes, Julie kissed him softly on the cheek. 'Not everyone,' she smiled, and together they walked up the steps and into the school.

The bustling, early morning corridor fell silent as Ben entered. He felt a prickly heat on his cheeks as every eye in the place turned to look at him. Keeping his head down, he walked towards his locker.

Suddenly, two figures stepped out in front of him. Ben recognised them as JT and Cash, two bullies who had made his life a misery when he was younger. He braced himself for their abuse.

But to his surprise, they began to slowly clap their hands. Soon, kids on both sides of the hallway joined in. Within moments, the applause had spread all the way along the corridor.

'You've helped a lot of people in this school,' JT said. He smiled, and for once it looked like a real one. 'You're all right, Tennyson.'

Ben smiled back. Yesterday had been pretty awful, but today

was already shaping up to be a whole lot better!

Many miles away, Bivalvan still dangled in his cocoon. A sound in the darkness startled him.

'Hello? Are you the Plumbers?' he called into the dark cave. 'Ben said you'd be here quickly, but I didn't think –'

He stopped as a shadowy figure stepped into view. His red shell went suddenly pale.

'Aggregor,' he spluttered.

'No one escapes me, Bivalvan,' growled the figure. His energy staff crackled menacingly, and a moment later, Bivalvan's screams echoed around the cavern.

A crowd is amazed by Humungousaur

Kevin has some news for Ben

Ben's alien action has been tracked

Ben is stuck behind bars

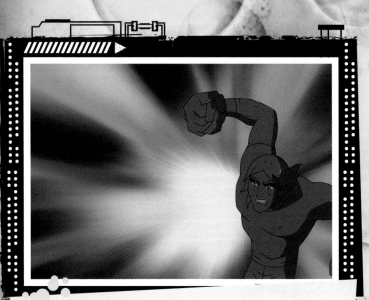

Kevin turns into living rock

Bivalvan turns on the taps

It's back to school for Ben

Aggregor confronts Bivalvan

The peace in the park is shattered

Angry Rath makes an entrance

Echo Echo prepares to go human

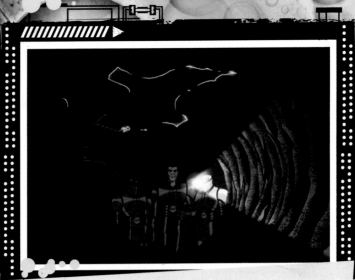

The Forever Knights explore a sewer

Film-fan Ben has fun at the movies

Humungousaur and Kevin drop in

Ben takes a call and is on his way

Lodestar comes to the rescue

DUPED

CHAPTER ONE

TANK BATTLE

It was a sunny afternoon in Bellwood. In the park, two old men sat on a bench, throwing bread to the pigeons.

A low rumbling sound came from along the street and the two men turned to see what it was. Their jaws fell open when they spotted a large, black tank crawling along the road towards them.

The lines of the tank were smooth and curved. It moved on caterpillar tracks and had an enormous gun at the front.

The ground vibrated and the two men watched on, amazed,

as the tank trundled by them and stopped outside the museum.

Inside the vehicle, two Forever Knights worked the controls, taking aim with the tank's plasma cannon.

'Right then, we go in fast, grab what we came for, and get out,' instructed the first knight.

'Charging the cannon now,' replied the second. 'This'll rip that old door open like it was made of tissue paper!'

SCREEEEECH!

Daylight suddenly filled the

dark cockpit of the tank, as two black claws tore the metal roof away. A seven-foot-tall tiger-like alien stood on the tank, his muscles bulging, the Omnitrix logo on his chest glowing green. He was Ben's alien Rath, and – as always – he was very angry.

'Let me tell you something, Forever Knights!' he roared. 'Nobody's rippin' open *nothin*', except Rath!'

Screaming in terror, the knights raised their handheld laser blasters and fired. The energy bolts bounced harmlessly off Rath's striped skin.

'That's your first mistake,' he bellowed. 'When you shoot Rath, it just makes Rath mad!'

Briiiiing, briiiing.

Rath paused, mid-roar, and reached for his mobile phone. He held it between his thumb and index finger, being careful not to crush it to dust.

'Hello?' he said, in a voice that was suddenly warm and friendly.

'Ben, where are you?' hissed Gwen. 'Julie's in the middle of her first set!'

In the background, Rath could hear a tennis ball being *thwacked* back and forth, and the applause of a crowd. 'Let me tell you something,

Gwen Tennyson,' he growled.
'I was on my way there when I saw
this tank outside the museum and –'

'I don't care!' Gwen snapped,
interrupting him. 'Get here.'

The phone went dead. Rath
shook his head. 'That was harsh,'
he muttered. 'Now!' he said, raising
his voice back to a roar. 'Where
were we?'

Rath turned back to the tank,
but found it empty. The Forever
Knights had run away when he
wasn't looking.

Exploding with rage, Rath
used his claws to slice through the
tank as if it were made of soggy
cardboard. With a snarl, he hoisted
the wreckage above his head and
tossed it into the pond right behind
where the two old men were sitting.

'What?' he growled, noticing their shocked expression. 'It was already busted!'

On all sides of the stadium, hundreds of onlookers watched as Julie picked up the ball and prepared to serve.

'Welcome back to the National Junior Tennis Championships,' said a voice from the tannoy system. 'Where an exciting semi-final round is in progress. Newcomer Julie Yamamoto is at match point.'

The stadium fell silent as Julie bounced the ball a few times. On the other side of the net, her opponent bounced from foot to foot, ready to leap into action.

Just then, a wave of gasps and

cheers swept through the audience, breaking Julie's concentration. Cameras flashed and people leapt to their feet as a familiar figure strode down the steps towards his seat.

'Hold on, there's a celebrity in the crowd!' said the announcer. 'The famous teen media sensation, Ben Tennyson.'

The crowd went wild, surging forwards as they tried their best to get Ben's autograph.

'Pardon. Hi. 'Scuse me,' Ben said, pushing his way through the throng until he reached Kevin and Gwen. With a sharp yank, Gwen pulled him down in his seat, and scowled at the crowd until they all backed off and sat down.

On the court, Julie shook her head. Throwing the ball into the air, she hit it with her racquet.

'Fault!' announced the umpire, as the ball struck the net. Julie shook her head again, really annoyed at herself.

'Sorry!' Ben shouted. Gwen elbowed him sharply in the ribs.

Julie picked up another ball. She tossed it into the air, then brought the racquet up and over in a devastating overhead smash.

The other player didn't stand a chance. She dived wildly, her own racquet outstretched, but the ball was already past her.

'Game, set, match,' announced the umpire, and the audience applauded.

Ben, Gwen and Kevin were the first to congratulate the winner.

'Nice game, Julie!' smiled Ben. Julie did not smile back.

'How would you know?'

Clutching her racquet, she turned and stomped off towards the changing rooms.

'What? What'd I say?' Ben mumbled quietly.

'It's what you *did*, Ben,'
Gwen told him. 'You were late, and
when you finally showed up, you
made a big entrance and blew her
concentration.'

'I can't help it if I'm famous,'
shrugged Ben. 'Right?'

Gwen's angry glare burned
straight into him.

'I'm sorry, it won't happen
again,' he said, flatly.

'It better not,' Gwen warned
him. 'The finals are in exactly three
hours. That should be enough time

for you to figure out how to make this up to Julie.'

With that, she turned and stomped off, just as Julie had done. Ben and Kevin watched her go.

'Any suggestions?' Ben asked, when his cousin was out of earshot.

'Yeah, *there's* a plan,' said Kevin, with a snort. 'Ask *me* for girlfriend advice.'

CARAW! CARAW!

A flock of black crows sat in the lair of the Forever Knights, watching the scene with their black, beady eyes.

Two knights stood side by side, their heads bowed. Before them stood their leader, King Urien. On his face was an angry sneer.

'You have revealed our plans to our enemies *and* lost our only plasma-beam tank,' snarled King Urien. 'You must explain yourselves.'

One of the knights spoke. 'We didn't *lose* it, sire. It's outside the museum. Ben Tennyson tore it to tiny pieces, but ...' His voice faded beneath Urien's gaze.

'We know *exactly* where ...' the other knight continued, before he, too, realised the King was not happy. He chuckled, nervously. 'Actually, it's almost *funny* when you think about it.'

King Urien clearly did not think it was funny. Raising a hand, he unleashed a crackling bolt of energy at the first knight. A melted mess of armour landed on the other side of the room with a **clang**. At once, the crows began pecking at the gaps in the scorched metal.

King Urien turned to the knight left behind. 'I can see that if I'm ever to restore the honour of the Forever Knights, it will require a more ... *hands-on* approach.'

CHAPTER TWO

THE TENNYSON TRIPLETS

Ben and Kevin hurried along one of the stadium's corridors, rushing to catch up with Gwen.

'C'mon, Gwen, wait up!' Ben cried after her.

Gwen stopped, folded her arms, and turned to face them. She tapped her foot as Ben spoke.

'OK, so I was a little late,' he admitted. 'I was kind of *busy*.'

'This tournament is important to her,' Gwen told him.

Kevin stepped forward. 'If we're doing *important*, maybe we could try figuring out why those Forever Knights were trying to bust into that museum.'

'Forever Knights, like that's a big riddle,' Gwen snapped. 'They're trying to steal alien technology so they can slay dragons, or take over the world, or whatever.'

'So now we just *ignore* them when they try to take over the world?' Kevin demanded.

'They're always taking over the world!' Gwen said. 'But this is Julie's first big tennis tournament.

We should be supporting her. Especially Ben ...'

Gwen stared at her cousin in horror. He had his mobile phone out, and was jabbing at the keys.

'*What* are you doing?' she asked him.

Ben shrugged. 'I was thinking that while we're waiting around, I could go and catch *Sumo Slammers: The Movie*.'

Gwen's scowl deepened.

Ben frowned. 'What? It's opening *today*,' said Ben. And there's a two o'clock show just a few streets from –'

Gwen's hand was suddenly over his mouth. 'No,' she said, flatly, before removing her hand again.

'But it's *Sumo Slammers*!' Ben whined. 'In 3D!'

'Ben ...'

'It's their first live action movie! Everyone knows live action is better than cartoons!'

'Benjamin Kirby Tennyson!' Gwen snarled. 'Don't even think about it. You can't be in two places at once!'

And with a final scowl, she turned and walked away, with Kevin hurrying along at her heels.

A smile crept slowly across Ben's face as an idea hit him. 'Or maybe I can ...'

After checking the coast was clear, Ben snuck into the men's toilets. Empty, just as he'd hoped. Activating the Ultimatrix, he transformed into Echo Echo. A second later, he'd split into three identical-looking clones.

'OK, boys, set your Ultimatrix to "human" and follow my lead,' said the first Echo Echo.

A blinding flash lit up the bathroom. When it faded, three Ben Tennysons stood there. They all looked at each other in surprise.

'I didn't really think that was going to work,' said the first Ben.

'Why not? You're a smart guy,' said another. His voice was softer and he seemed much more sensitive than Ben usually was.

'I dunno,' said the third Ben,

his face pulled into a sneer. 'I think you're kind of a dope.'

'Yeah? Well this dope's going to see *Sumo Slammers*!'

The sensitive Ben rested a hand on the first Ben's shoulder. 'You work hard. You deserve a treat every now and again,' he said. 'Tell you what, I'll go with Kevin and keep an eye out for those Forever Knights.'

'Perfect!' The first Ben turned to the third. 'And you ...'

'What?'

'You could watch Julie play in the tournament,' Sensitive Ben suggested. 'After all, she's always so nice to us, it's only right that –'

'Yeah, fine, whatever,' the rude Ben shrugged, bored of the other two. He headed over to the door and left the room.

Gwen was in the corridor, hunting him down. She stormed over when she spotted him. 'Where have you been?' she demanded. 'Julie's match is about to start!'

'I'm *here*,' he scowled. 'Why don't you put a sock in it?'

Gwen was shocked. 'Whoa. What's wrong with you?'

'I'm Ben *classic*,' he told her. 'Miss me?'

Rolling her eyes, Gwen turned and headed towards the spectator area, with Rude Ben walking lazily along behind. Kevin arrived just in time to see them head through the door. Munching on a hot dog, he moved to follow, but a tap on his shoulder stopped him.

'Hello, Kevin,' said Sensitive

Ben, smiling warmly. 'I hope I didn't keep you waiting.'

Kevin paused, mid-chew. He looked at the door to the spectator area, then back to Ben. 'Didn't I just see you with Gwen?'

'I guess so,' admitted Sensitive Ben. 'Now then, didn't you want to go and investigate the Forever Knights robbery?'

'Yeah ... but Gwen's pretty mad at you. You'd better –'

Ben patted Kevin on the arm. 'Gwen might seem tough, but her heart is as big as all outdoors,' he said. 'She'll forgive me.'

'*Gwen* will forgive you?' spluttered Kevin, almost choking on his hot dog. 'Gwen Tennyson?'

'The mission's important to you, and you're important to me, my friend,' said Ben. 'Let's go.'

Kevin crammed the rest of his hot dog in his mouth and shrugged. 'Something's definitely wrong here,' he mumbled. 'But so far it's working out for me.'

Kevin and Sensitive Ben were barely out of the corridor when the door to the men's toilets creaked open and the other Ben popped his head out. He smiled when he saw the coast was clear.

'Julie's covered. Gwen's covered. Kevin's covered,' he said, scampering along the corridor towards the main exit. 'And I'm off to the movies!'

Half a mile away, deep below the city, three armoured figures marched through the sewers. King Urien led the way, two of his knights by his side. One of them held a torch, lighting the way ahead. The other carried a strange, circular device, with sharp prongs on its base.

King Urien stopped by the wall of a sewer tunnel. With a nod, he motioned for the knight with the device to attach it to the damp, stone wall.

As the metal prongs dug into the stone, a colourful display on its front began to flash.

Bleep! Bleep! Bleep!

The three men shielded their eyes as the device began to crackle with energy. It spun like a Catherine wheel, creating a circular swirl of energy that sliced through the solid stone. In moments, a long, round passageway had been carved into the rock.

'Onward, my knights!' King Urien commanded. 'This time, nothing will stop us from gaining supreme power!' And with that,

he stepped through the hole in the
wall, and into the darkness that
waited beyond.

CHAPTER THREE

NAUGHTY AND NICE

Julie looked across to her opponent on the other side of the net, and cleared her mind of everything except winning.

'GO JULIE!'

OK, *almost* everything. Ben was cheering so loudly that he was distracting. And the way he was jumping up and down and waving a giant foam finger around wasn't helping, either.

'*Whoooo!* Julie Yamamoto is number one, baby!' shouted Ben from the front row of the audience.

'Whoo! Whoo! Whoo!'

Grabbing his arm, Gwen
pulled him back down into his seat.
'You're embarrassing her,' she
scolded.

'My bad,' he said, with a
shrug. Shoving Gwen's arm away,
he stood up and marched up the
steps until he was in full view of the
rest of the crowd. 'Hey, other girl,'
he cried, pointing towards Julie's
opponent. 'You're a terrible tennis
player, and my girlfriend's going to
thrash you!'

Julie's opponent scowled
across at her. Up in the stands, a
crowd had gathered around Ben.
News reporters, photographers and
several cute female fans flocked
around him.

The tennis umpire did not look impressed. 'What's happening up there?' he asked Julie, his face an angry scowl.

'Uh, that's my ... boyfriend,' Julie admitted.

The umpire shook his head. 'You must be *very* proud,' he said.

Up on the steps, Ben was loving the attention. He smirked as a microphone was shoved right in front of him.

'Ben, what do you think about Will Harangue off the TV?' asked the reporter. 'He says that you're a big menace.'

'Yeah?' said Ben, yawning. 'And I say TV's old news. Sorry, man, you know it's true.'

A teenage girl with long blonde hair squeezed in through a gap in the crowd. She blushed as Ben turned to look at her. 'I'm your *biggest fan*,' she told him.

'Well, that makes two of us!' Rude Ben replied.

'Is that really your girlfriend on the court?' the girl asked. She twirled her hair, nervously.

Ben raised an eyebrow. 'Hey, things change,' he began, before a bolt of pink energy zapped him on his head. 'Ow!' he moaned, turning to face his cousin. 'What?'

PEEEEEEEEEEEEEEEEP!

A whistle silenced the crowd. The umpire glared up at them. 'Would ... you ... *mind*?' he growled.

Ben leaned in and whispered into the girl's ear. 'We'll talk later,' he told her, before raising a thumb to the umpire. 'Sorry, ref!'

As the audience settled down, Julie tried to turn her attention back to the game. Clearing her mind, she took her position and served.

A few streets away, Kevin's car was outside the museum. Inside, Kevin and Sensitive Ben kept an eye on the front door.

'Whatever the Knights were after, you stopped them from getting it,' said Kevin. He paused, realising that Ben was staring at him. 'What?' he asked. 'Do I have hot dog on my face?'

'No,' Ben replied. 'I'm just thinking about how long we've known one another.'

'Why?'

'Because I don't think we've ever talked about our *feelings*,' said Ben. 'About how we're *friends* now, but we were enemies.'

'I talk about my feelings all the time,' Kevin pointed out. 'Like when I'm mad. Or hungry. Or when I have to go to the bathroom.'

'Not to mention that there are probably still problems from when you hacked into the Omnitrix and turned into a monster,' Ben said, cheerfully. 'Which, though I didn't want to say anything at the time, made you *really* hard to be around. 'Not that I blame you,' he added, quickly, 'since it was all my fault that things went so badly wrong.'

Kevin sighed, turned away and stared out through the side window of the car. He hoped the Forever Knights showed up soon, because he'd much rather be attacked than have to listen to Ben babble one more word.

Back at the stadium, the players were taking a break. Gwen

leaned over the railing around the court, offering support to Julie.

'I can't believe I blew that last shot,' Julie groaned.

'It's OK, you're still ahead,' said Gwen. 'Just remember, I'm here for you. Kevin's here for you. Ben's here for ...'

They both looked up to the top of the stairs, where Ben was still chatting to his female admirers. Gwen realised, too, that Kevin was nowhere to be seen.

'OK,' she sighed. 'Make that one out of three.'

'What is *wrong* with him?' asked Julie, squeezing the handle of her racquet tightly.

Gwen didn't know what was wrong with Ben, but she was going to give him a piece of her mind.

Striding up the steps, she shooed the girls away. Only the blonde-haired one remained.

When she showed no sign of moving, Gwen fired a bolt of energy from her fingertip. It nudged the girl backwards and out of sight.

Furious, Gwen turned on her cousin. 'All Julie wanted was a little support, but *nooo*. You're too busy chatting with other girls.'

Gwen marched back down the steps to her seat. Ben shouted after her, 'Come on! It's just a dumb old tennis game! Besides, she was supposed to lose, anyway.'

Everyone in the audience turned to look at Ben, horrified. On the court, Julie tried to hide her tears. 'Sheesh,' Ben muttered. 'Sound *really* carries in here.'

Half a mile away, unaware of the trouble his doubles were causing, Film-fan Ben sat in the cinema, stuffing popcorn into his mouth. Behind his 3D glasses, his eyes sparkled with excitement, as the characters on the screen leapt into action.

As one, the entire audience jumped to their feet, raised their hands above their heads and cheered. 'It's slammer time!'

Below the city, King Urien and his knights burned another tunnel through the rock. They marched along it, Urien leading the way, the others following just behind.

As they neared the end, one of the knights stepped forwards. He held out a map for his leader to see. 'Sire, I'm not certain I know how to read this,' he admitted.

Urien stopped at another wall. He touched it with his gloved hand. This was the way, he was certain.

'I have little patience for failure, Knight,' he glowered. He pointed to a spot in the centre of the wall. 'Plant the device!'

The knight hurried to follow the King's order. Urien allowed himself a grim smile. Soon, he would have what he had come for. And then the whole world would tremble at his name!

CHAPTER FOUR

THE SECRET ARMOUR

Kevin gripped the steering wheel so hard his knuckles turned white. He wished he'd brought earplugs.

'... and, of course, what with your relationship with my cousin Gwen,' Sensitive Ben prattled on, 'you and I might someday be related, which could get kinda –'

'Ben!' Kevin snapped loudly.

'Uh huh?'

'You've always been kinda girly, but today you're really creeping me out.'

Ben gently patted Kevin's arm. 'It's alright. I understand. And I am truly sorry.'

'*Stop understanding!*' Kevin cried, pulling his arm away. 'Stop apologising! Stop *talking about your feelings*! I just want to find some Forever Knights to fight!'

Ben stroked his chin, thoughtfully. 'Hmm,' he said, nodding. 'Interesting.'

Kevin raised a fist, angrily. 'Cut that out!'

Ben opened his mouth to reply,

but a sudden muffled explosion stopped him. 'Is that a deterion energy mine?'

'Yup,' said Kevin, leaping out of the car. 'They're hugely dangerous. They can burn a hole through ten feet of rock ... it must be the knights! We'd better suit up.'

Bending down, Kevin placed his hand against a metal manhole cover. Absorbing its properties, his body became as strong as iron.

Meanwhile, Ben had activated the Ultimatrix. His body grew and his skin became thick and orange.

'Humungousaur!' he sang in a high, wobbly voice, just like an opera singer.

For a moment, Kevin was too shocked to react. Finally, he said, '*Never* do that again.'

'Just trying it out,' smiled the dino-alien. 'Can you tell which way they're coming from?'

CRRRRRRCK!

The ground beneath them began to split and crack. Kevin looked up at Humungousaur. 'Yes,' he said, before the road opened wide and swallowed them both up.

THUUUBOOM!

They landed in a tunnel, barely large enough for Humungousaur to stand up in. Three armoured men stood before them. 'Who dares intrude?' demanded the leader.

'It's Ben Tennyson, sire,' said one of King Urien's knights. 'The alien-man. And his servant.'

'Oh, now I'm a "servant",' grimaced Kevin.

'I'm sure he didn't mean to hurt your feelings,' Humungousaur told him.

'Destroy them!' barked King Urien. The two knights quickly took aim with their energy lances.

Kevin yelped with pain as a blast scorched his metal skin. Hurling himself sideways, he took cover behind Humungousaur.

'I think they're being hurtful on purpose,' the dino-alien said. He failed to notice King Urien sneaking away, two energy mines tucked under his arm.

Back at the cinema, Film-fan Ben was on his third tub of popcorn. He watched as on-screen, two bulky men in big nappies slammed each other into walls.

Ben grinned, unable to contain his excitement. 'I just love a good fight scene!'

Laser fire streaked along the tunnel, punching holes in the stone around Humungousaur. Behind him, Kevin kept low, trying to avoid another fiery blast.

'Ben, *do* something!' he yelled.

'Why me?'

'Because you're a giant, indestructible dinosaur!'

'OK,' replied Humungousaur, 'but shouldn't we try to work together so that we both feel involved in the plan?'

'Forget it!' Kevin cried. He squatted down and tucked his knees up against his chest. 'Just throw me.'

'OK!' replied Humungousaur, cheerfully. Snatching up Kevin in one hand, he hurled him like a bowling ball along the corridor. Before the knights could leap to safety, Kevin smashed through them, sending them crashing to the ground like skittles.

Kevin stood up, then struggled to keep his balance as the walls of the tunnel shook. Another energy mine was being used nearby.

'Let's go!' Kevin urged, hurrying along the passageway.

Humungousaur moved to follow him, then yelped with pain as he bumped his head against a low-hanging metal pipe. With a flash of green light, he turned back into Ben.

'Owwww!' he sobbed, clutching his forehead.

Kevin glowered at him. 'Why are you being such a baby?' he asked, striding off.

'Well,' said Ben, 'it *hurt*!'

King Urien stalked the halls of the museum, until he finally arrived at the exhibit he was looking for. An imposing Aztec statue towered above him. It was made of bronze and gold, and stood almost as high as the ceiling. Directly in front of it, a gold necklace was on display inside a glass case. Urien spotted the large red stone in the necklace's centre.

KA-RASH!

His armoured fist shattered the display case. Eagerly, he reached inside and tore the stone free of the chain. 'It's mine!' he gasped, barely able to believe it. 'After all this time, it's mine!'

'Excuse me, sir,' said a polite voice from behind him. Ben and Kevin climbed through the hole Urien had blasted in the museum floor. Ben smiled as he approached. 'The signs clearly say "Do not touch the exhibits".'

'*Signs?*' Kevin spat. 'That's the best you got? Where's the usual smack talk?'

'I didn't think we needed to be insulting,' Ben replied.

Unnoticed by the boys, Urien was inserting the stolen jewel into an opening on the statue. As the villain watched, the statue began to open up, revealing a hollow, man-sized opening inside.

At last, Kevin realised that Urien was up to no good. He turned in time to see the statue fold itself around the King. With a series of metallic clanks, Urien turned to reveal that the statue was, in fact, a giant suit of high-tech armour.

'We should talk about this later,' said Kevin, quietly.

Ben nodded. 'Uh huh.'

'This is Toltech Battle Armour,' boomed Urien's voice from inside the statue. 'A little parting gift left with the ancient Aztecs by a race of aliens.'

With a *whirring* of machinery, Urien advanced. Kevin dived to safety, but Ben was slower to react. A heavy bronze fist smashed into him, sending him toppling backwards into a display of old metal shields.

Kevin was at his side in moments. 'How could you let your guard down like that?' he asked.

Ben shook his head, trying to clear away the cobwebs. 'I'm not myself today.'

'Yeah? Well, pull it together,' he said. Absorbing the copper from one of the shields, Kevin stood up and faced off against the towering battle armour. 'OK, tin man,' he growled, narrowing his eyes. 'It's you and me!'

And with that, he attacked.

CHAPTER FIVE

THREE INTO ONE

Ben lay on the floor, nursing his bruises and watching Kevin attack the robotic battle armour. Kevin was tough, but the fight wasn't going his way.

Ben reached for his phone. Kevin was right. It was time to pull himself together.

Dialling his own phone number, he hit conference call, and waited for the answers.

'Hello?' came one voice.

'Hello?' came the other.

'I hate to interrupt everyone's evening,' Ben said. 'Is everyone having a good time?'

'This movie's awesome!' crowed one Ben.

The other sniffed. 'It's OK.'

'Well, we're fighting an ancient alien battle robot, and we're not doing too well ...' Sensitive Ben told them. As if to prove the point, Kevin went whizzing through the air, screaming.

The other two Bens both spoke at exactly the same time. 'On our way!'

Minutes later, Rude Ben and Film-fan Ben arrived outside the museum, both out of breath from the effort of running so far.

With a **boom**, the front doors of the museum suddenly flew open. Kevin and Sensitive Ben erupted from inside. They were running as fast as they could.

'Go! Go! Go!' cried Kevin.

'I'm going, I'm going, I'm going!' replied Sensitive Ben.

Kevin raced ahead, easily outpacing Ben. He didn't slow when he passed the other Bens. 'If I wasn't running for my life, I'd totally demand an explanation,' he called back over his shoulder.

'Sumo Slammers opened today,' began one.

'We were trying to be sensitive to everyone's needs,' explained another.

'And just what is it to you?' snarled the third.

'Again,' Kevin shouted, not in the least bit interested, 'running for my life!'

Suddenly, the front of the museum crumbled and King Urien stepped out, still encased in his Toltech Battle Armour. He gave a low chuckle when he spotted the trio of Bens.

'Three of you? That's great, the more the merrier!'

It was Film-fan Ben who stepped forward first. 'Boys,' he said, looking at each of his clones. 'It's Slammer Time!'

Three green flashes lit up the street, as three equally incredible transformations took place.

Sensitive Ben became the frosty, blue, ghost-like apparition, Big Chill.

The Ben who'd been to the movies changed into the squat, reptile-like Upchuck.

Rude Ben swelled up like a balloon, becoming Cannonbolt.

Spinning quickly into a ball, Cannonbolt launched himself towards the towering battle armour. Upchuck was already on the attack though, spewing a thick stream of yucky, gooey yellow slime at the robotic suit.

When Cannonbolt rolled over the sludge, he began to slip and slide. He cried out as he missed his target completely, and crashed at full speed into a nearby tree.

Taking to the sky, Big Chill ejected an icy blast of Arctic air from his lungs. The cloud rolled towards its target, but just before it hit, Upchuck scampered in front of it, on his way to help Cannonbolt. The cloud froze Upchuck, mid-run, in a block of solid ice.

'Sorry!' cried Big Chill. He was so busy apologising he failed to notice Urien's battle suit take a swing at him. The metal fist swatted him from the air and bounced him hard against the pavement.

HISSSSSSSSSS!

The ice around Upchuck melted, as he vomited up another mouthful of corrosive goo. 'This is a lot less fun than I thought it would be,' Upchuck grumbled.

'You're telling me,' groaned Cannonbolt. They both looked up to find Kevin running towards them, ready to join the fight again.

'Hold him off, Kevin,' Upchuck shouted. 'We'll be right with you.'

Pausing only to absorb the strength of a stone statue, Kevin raced back into battle with the Aztec armour, giving the Bens the breathing space they needed.

Big Chill limped over to join the other two. 'Time for a meeting of the minds,' he suggested, and all three of them activated their Omnitrix.

'Echo Echo!' they cried, as they each became identical copies of the little white alien. Quickly, they merged together, before transforming back into a single, solitary Ben Tennyson.

CRASH!

Kevin landed heavily on the ground beside him. His stone covering was cracked and chipped. 'Your turn,' he said with a groan.

Ben nodded and raced forwards, just as King Urien clanked across the street to meet him. Ben activated the Ultimatrix one more time, and transformed into one of his newer aliens.

'Lodestar!' he cried, as he became the magnetically powered black and yellow alien.

Urien swung down with a punch, but Lodestar was one step ahead of him. With the wave of a magnetic hand he held the giant metal fist in place. Urien fought to free the arm, but it was no use.

'I can't move!' Urien wailed.
'What black magic is this?'

'No magic, just my natural
magnetism,' Lodestar replied.
Raising his other hand, Lodestar hit
the armour with a magnetic blast.
The armour began to glow yellow.

CLANK!

A metal bin suddenly flew
through the air and slammed into
the now-magnetised metal of the
battle armour.

CLANK!

A road sign was torn from the

pavement. It hit King Urien hard, staggering him.

KABLAAAM!

Kevin's car lifted into the air. It flipped twice, before smashing into the armour at terrific speed.

Kevin almost cried with shock, when he saw the front of his car buckle as it hit the ground. 'Every ... time,' he sobbed.

Lodestar pointed both hands at the armour and fired two magnetic blasts. For a moment, the armour groaned and creaked. Then, with a deafening *screech*, the metal tore into pieces, leaving Urien completely exposed.

The king plunged to the ground. From flat on his back, he saw the broken chunks of the battle suit come plummeting towards him.

The metal rained down on him,
covering him completely.

Lodestar changed back into
Ben. Prodding the mound of metal
with his foot, he said, 'Rest in
pieces.' He smiled, then turned to
Kevin. 'Hey,' he said. 'You're *totally*
right about the smack-talking!'

Later, Ben, Kevin and Gwen
sat with Julie in the empty stadium.
Julie held a large gold trophy.
'I'm glad you won your

tournament, Julie,' said Ben, sheepishly.

'Yeah, thanks,' Julie replied. 'Ben, I know you were off fighting bad guys. I was upset, but I guess that's the deal when you decide to date a superhero.'

Ben smiled at her. 'Julie, I promise I'll make it up to you. Whatever you want to do, I'm there. Just name it.'

Julie thought for a moment. 'Well, maybe we could go and see *Sumo Slammers: The Movie* together some time.'

Ben chewed his lip. 'Actually, I, uh, already saw it.'

'When?'

'Um ... during your match.'

Julie leapt to her feet, furious. 'Well!' she cried, grabbing her trophy. 'That's just ... *ooooh*!'

She stormed off. Gwen was quick to follow her. 'Nice,' she scowled, pushing past her cousin.

Kevin, too, stood up. 'Man,' he muttered, to Ben, following the girls, 'you are *so* insensitive.'

Ben slumped with his head in his hands and sighed. Kevin was right. He *was* insensitive.

Some of the time, at least!